P9-BIC-604

THE UNTAMED WORLD

Whooping Cranes

Karen Dudley

RSVP

RAINTREE
STECK-VAUGHN
PUBLISHERS
The Steck-Vaughn Company

Austin, Texas

Published by Raintree Steck-Vaughn Publishers, an imprint of Steck-Vaughn Company.

Library of Congress Cataloging-in-Publication Data
Dudley, Karen.
      Whooping Cranes / Karen Dudley.
         p.   cm. -- (The Untamed world)
      Includes bibliographical references (p. 63) and index.
      Summary: Takes an in-depth look at the life of the whooping crane, from physical features to food and habitat, and describes the folklore surrounding cranes.
      ISBN 0-8172-4564-2
      1. Whooping crane--Juvenile literature.   [1. Whooping crane.]
I. Title. II. Series.
QL696.G84D83 1997
598.3'1--dc20
                                      96-21288
                                        CIP
                                        AC

Printed and bound in Canada
1234567890 01 00 99 98 97

Project Editor
Lauri Seidlitz
Design and Illustration
Warren Clark
Project Coordinator
Amanda Woodrow
Raintree Steck-Vaughn Publishers Editor
Kathy DeVico
Copyeditor
Janice Parker
Layout
Chris Bowerman

Consultants
Ernie Kuyt, retired whooping crane expert from the Canadian Wildlife Service

Tom Stehn, United States Fish and Wildlife Service, Aransas National Wildlife Refuge
Acknowledgments
The publisher wishes to thank Warren Rylands for inspiring this series.

Special thanks to the International Crane Foundation, and David Jones at the International Shotokan Karate Federation

Photograph Credits

Calgary Zoological Society: pages 27 (Chris Junck), 10, 22; **Corel Corporation**: pages 17, 43 bottom; **Rob Curtis/The Early Birder**: cover, pages 4, 12, 32, 37, 43 top, 59; **International Crane Foundation**: pages 5, 6, 7, 9, 15, 23, 25, 26, 28, 36, 38, 40, 42, 44, 45, 56, 60, 61; **Ivy Images**: page 8 (Don Johnston); **Ernie Kuyt**: pages 16, 21, 24, 29, 31, 41, 54, 55; **Stouffer Productions**: page 20; **Waterhen Film Productions**: pages 14, 18, 30 (Robert J. Long).

Contents

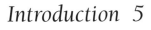

Introduction

Whooping cranes are the tallest—and one of the loudest—birds in North America.

Opposite: The whooping crane has become a symbol for wildlife conservation. Conservation programs rescued North America's whooping crane population from near extinction in 1940.

Whooping cranes usually migrate in pairs or small family groups.

KERLOO! KERLEEOO! The trumpeting call of a whooping crane echoes across the marshy meadows. It is an unmistakable sound. Whooping cranes are the tallest—and one of the loudest—birds in North America. Their name comes from their loud, whooping call. Whooping cranes, or whoopers, are water-loving birds. In coastal Mexico they are called *Viejos del Agua*, which means "Old Men of the Water."

In this book, you will find out how birds as large as whooping cranes are able to fly. You will learn how wild whoopers live and raise their young in their marshy habitat. You can also follow along as whooping cranes travel an amazing journey of over 2,485 miles (4,000 km)! Finally, you will discover how, after almost 60 years of conservation efforts, whooping cranes are coming back from the brink of extinction.

Features

Whoopers have long legs to keep their bodies above water as they search for food.

Opposite: Rust-colored juvenile whooping cranes do not turn white until their second autumn after hatching.

It is easy to spot the whoopers feeding with this group of sandhill cranes.

North America has only two species of cranes—whooping cranes and sandhill cranes. Although both species have a red patch on the tops of their heads, it is easy to tell the adults of the two types of cranes apart. Adult sandhill cranes are brownish-gray, while adult whooping cranes are white, with a row of black feathers on their wings.

Whooping cranes spend their days in ponds and other marshy areas. The cranes have evolved many features that help them live in this type of wet environment. They have long legs to keep their bodies above water as they search for food. Whooping cranes have strong beaks to help them eat animals such as crabs and snails. Like many other birds, whoopers also have several adaptations that enable them to fly.

Size

If you were to stand beside a full-grown whooper, it might be taller than you. At 5 feet (1.5 m) tall, whooping cranes are very large and powerful birds. When a whooper stretches its wings out, its wingspan can be up to 7 feet (2 m) across! Although male and female whooping cranes are about the same height, male whoopers are usually a little heavier. Male whooping cranes weigh about 16 pounds (7.3 kg), while female cranes weigh about 14 pounds (6.4 kg).

Unlike some birds, male and female whooping cranes have the same colors and markings.

LIFE SPAN

Whoopers living in the wild only live for about 30 years. Captive whooping cranes can live up to 40 years. Both captive and wild cranes may be killed by disease, drowning, predators, or injury. Wild cranes also face danger from natural disasters, such as hurricanes. In addition, wild whoopers may collide with power lines while flying and die.

Plumage

A bird's covering of feathers is known as its **plumage**. The whooping crane's plumage is snowy white, except for its primary feathers. These feathers, also called **primaries**, are the long, main feathers on a bird's wing. They are located on the tip of the wing. Except for some black around their beaks and the red markings on their heads, adult whoopers appear to be completely white when their wings are folded.

Legs and Feet

Whooping cranes belong to a group of birds known as shorebirds. This means that whoopers spend much of their time in **wetland** habitats. The cranes' long, thin legs keep their bodies from getting wet as they wade through ponds and marshes. They can also easily step over fallen logs or tall brush and grasses. Whooping cranes have unwebbed feet, which help support the birds when they walk or run through boggy areas. Whoopers take flight by running into the wind and pushing off into the air.

Adult whoopers cannot swim because their feet are unwebbed. Chicks, however, can swim until their legs grow enough to wade through their habitat.

Head and Beak

The red patch on a whooping crane's head is naked skin that is partially covered with thin, black, hairlike feathers. Whooping cranes use these patches of naked skin to communicate. By moving certain muscles, the cranes can vary the amount of bare skin that is displayed. A relaxed whooping crane will have a small red patch, while an excited or angry whooper will display a large red patch.

Whooping cranes have narrow heads, with strong, yellow-green beaks that are about 5.5 inches (14 cm) in length. With this long beak, a crane can dig up clams, mud shrimp, roots, and other foods. Along the side of the upper part of the beak, there are a number of small notches. These notches help the crane hang on to slippery prey such as fish. A whooper's beak is also used for defense against predators. If a predator comes too close, the crane can use its beak to stab at the intruder.

The whooping crane's beak is its main tool for finding, catching, and eating food.

Classification

Although only two species of cranes live in North America, there are 15 species of cranes around the world. Biologists believe that whoopers are most closely related to the Red-crowned crane (*Grus japonensis*) of northeast Asia.

SPECIES

Species	Latin Name	Where They Live
Black-crowned crane	*Balearica pavonina*	Africa
Black-necked crane	*Grus nigricollis*	Tibet and China
Blue crane	*Grus paradisea*	South Africa and Namibia
Brolga crane	*Grus rubicunda*	Australia
Common crane	*Grus grus*	Europe and Asia
Demoiselle crane	*Grus virgo*	Northwest Africa, Asia, Crimea
Gray-crowned crane	*Balearica regulorum*	Southern Africa
Hooded crane	*Grus monacha*	Japan, China, and Russia
Red-crowned crane	*Grus japonensis*	Japan, China, and Russia
Sandhill crane	*Grus canadensis*	North America
Sarus crane	*Grus antigone*	India, IndoChina, and Australia
Siberian crane	*Grus leucogeranus*	Eastern China and Russia
Wattled crane	*Grus carunculatus*	Southern and eastern Africa
White-naped crane	*Grus vipio*	Russia
Whooping crane	*Grus americana*	North America

Adaptations for Flight

Whooping cranes have several features that help them fly. All other flying birds share these adaptations.

Feathers

A whooping crane feather is made up of many parallel branches, or barbs, that are attached to a central shaft. Each barb has hundreds of tiny hooks, called barbules, that stick together. When the barbs are locked together by the hooks, the feather is strong. It helps support the crane when it flies, and keeps the bird dry by shedding moisture. A bird's feathers also help regulate heat. They keep the bird warm or cool, depending on the weather.

When a whooper flies or hunts, the hooks may sometimes come apart, and the barbs may separate. To fix this, whooping cranes must spend a large part of their day cleaning and taking care of their feathers. This behavior is known as **preening**. When whoopers preen, they use their beaks like a comb. By drawing a feather between the upper and lower parts of its beak, a whooper may comb the barbs and barbules back together again.

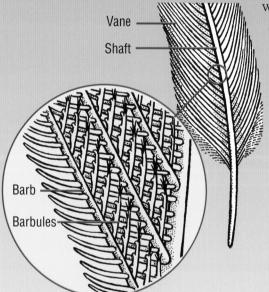

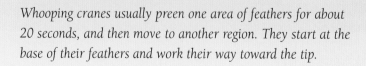

Whooping cranes usually preen one area of feathers for about 20 seconds, and then move to another region. They start at the base of their feathers and work their way toward the tip.

Skeleton

Most mammal bones are very heavy because they are solid or filled with marrow. If a whooping crane had heavy bones like a mammal, it would never get off the ground. Like most other birds, whoopers have a skeleton of thin, hollow bones. Many of these bones are joined together for added strength. This combination of lightness and strength helps support the cranes as they fly.

Although the rest of their skeleton is rigid, whooping cranes have very flexible necks. This is because cranes have many small bones in their neck. While mammals have seven neck bones, whooping cranes can have up to 20. This flexible neck allows a whooper to reach out and grab a snack, to preen its feathers, or to fold its neck and rest.

Carpal (wrist)

Skull

Phalanges (finger bones)

Vertebrae (neck bones)

Humerus

Scapula (shoulder blade)

Sternum (chest)

Phalanges (toe bones)

13

The Flock

The most common type of whooper flock is made up of a mated pair, with or without a chick.

Opposite: Unlike sandhill cranes, which can be seen in huge flocks of thousands of birds, whooping cranes live and migrate in pairs or small groups.

Once whooping cranes select their mates, the two cranes spend all of their time together. Whooping cranes mate for life. If one crane dies, however, the other will take a new mate.

There are two types of whooping crane flocks. The most common type of whooper flock is made up of a mated pair, with or without a chick. Adult cranes rarely interact with one another except during **territorial** disputes or migration.

Other flocks are formed from small groups of young cranes. Unlike adult cranes, young cranes do socialize with one another. These flocks may stay together for several months or even through the winter. Biologists believe this kind of flock provides a place for young whooping cranes to choose their mates.

Flock Composition

The most permanent kind of whooping crane flock is formed when an adult crane chooses its mate. The mated pair is considered a flock. If they are successful in hatching a chick, the youngster is also included in their flock. The small family group lives together on the summer, or nesting, grounds. When it is time to **migrate** south for the winter, the crane family makes the trip together. During migration a few paired or single cranes may join up with the family for a short time.

The crane chick stays with its parents throughout the autumn, winter, and during the following spring migration. Once the cranes reach the nesting grounds again, the young crane is left to survive on its own.

The second kind of flock is formed from young, or **subadult**, cranes. Subadult whoopers are cranes over one year old that have not yet mated. A whooper may join a subadult flock for a whole season, or only a few days. When subadult cranes leave the summer grounds in the fall, they usually migrate together. Flocks of ten birds have been reported, but groups of two to seven cranes are more common. Larger flocks may form briefly if a good food source is available.

On the winter grounds, subadults form small flocks along the edges of adult territories. They move around quite a bit, and are often chased off by adults defending their range. Young whoopers associate with other subadults until they are old enough to mate.

There are two flocks flying together in this formation—a mated pair on the right, and another mated pair with their offspring on the left.

Migrations

Whooping cranes migrate twice a year—once in the spring and again in the fall. They spend the fall and winter months in Texas at the Aransas National Wildlife Refuge and in coastal marshes near the refuge. In the spring and summer, they live in Wood Buffalo National Park in the Northwest Territories and Alberta, in Canada. The whoopers' migration route between these areas is over 2,485 miles (4,000 km) long.

In the spring, northern migration begins when warm winds begin to blow into the Aransas area from the Gulf of Mexico. As the temperature rises and the days become longer, whooping cranes begin to migrate north to their nesting grounds. The cranes do not all leave at once. Some leave in March, while most leave in April. A few cranes stay on until the first week in May. The migration of family flocks can take between 10 and 27 days. Subadult birds may take up to 40 days to complete the migration. After migrating north, the cranes spend the summer foraging for food and raising their chicks.

Most whoopers leave Wood Buffalo National Park sometime between mid-September and mid-October. Biologists believe that southern migration is triggered by many factors, including changing temperature and weather patterns, and a decrease in available food. After leaving Wood Buffalo National Park, the cranes visit their **staging area**, which is a place where cranes can eat a lot of food before their migration. Whoopers spend 1 to 5 weeks at their staging area before continuing their journey to Texas. Most whooping cranes arrive at their winter grounds near the Aransas National Wildlife Refuge by the end of November. Whooping cranes do not have a staging area when migrating north in the spring.

Whoopers in Flight

During migration, whoopers fly about 7.5 hours a day. They usually cover about 250 miles (400 km) in this time. Biologists recorded one whooping crane family that traveled 508 miles (818 km) in a single day!

Whooping cranes usually fly at about 35 miles (56 km) per hour. If the wind is blowing in the same direction they are traveling, the cranes can reach speeds of up to 66 miles (106 km) per hour. Whoopers like to migrate when the winds are blowing in the right direction, but they can also fly against the wind.

When flying, whooping cranes make use of **thermals**. These are columns or bubbles of warm air that rise up in the sky. By stretching out their wings, whoopers spiral up on these rising thermals. Like a glider plane, whoopers gain height by riding the thermals. On a good thermal, whooping cranes can rise up 726 yards (653 m) in just 2 minutes! This is twice as fast as a small airplane can rise. The cranes combine this thermal spiraling with downward gliding. When the thermal breaks up, they glide downward and forward until they meet another thermal.

By riding thermals and gliding, whooping cranes can fly easily without having to flap their wings. This helps them save energy for long flights.

Flying Formation

When three or more whooping cranes migrate together, they usually fly in a V-shaped formation or in a single line. In most cases, the whooper at the front of the formation is the largest adult. This adult helps to break the wind resistance for the others. In this way, younger or smaller cranes do not have to struggle against the wind, making it easier for them to keep up with the leader.

The V-formation is the most common flying formation. Cranes usually keep a distance of about 3.4 feet (1 m) between them when flying. Sometimes a young crane may fly more closely to an adult.

Communication

Whooping cranes communicate in many different ways. Complex dances help strengthen the bond between mates. Body language indicates a crane's mood. Whoopers also communicate with trumpeting calls.

Dancing and Pair-Bonding

In a subadult flock, young cranes meet and choose their mates. The pair begins its courtship by looking for food and resting together. Then they split off from the rest of the group to establish their own territory. When whoopers choose a mate, it is known as **pair-bonding**. This normally takes place on the winter grounds or during spring migration.

Dancing is an important part of the pair-bonding ritual. The whooping crane dance begins when one crane bows its head and flaps its wings to show off its black primary feathers. It then jumps into the air, its legs stiff and its head pointing to the sky. The other crane runs to its mate, nodding its head and flapping its wings. Then both whoopers leap up and down, bow their heads, and stretch their wings. The dancing lasts for several minutes at a time.

Whooping cranes may dance together at any time of the year. Most of the dancing takes place as the cranes migrate to their summer nesting grounds and build nests.

Body Language

Whooping cranes show aggression through body language. A whooper warns off intruders by strutting around with stiff legs. It raises its wings to show off its black primary feathers. The crane may also arch its neck so that the bright red patch on its head faces forward. Sometimes a crane even preens in front of an intruder. As the whooper combs its feathers, it does not take its eyes off the other crane. When a crane backs down, it tries to make itself look smaller. It bends its neck and holds its feathers close to its body.

With raised wings and stiff legs, this crane is trying to warn off an intruder. This is a common nest-defense posture.

Calling

Whooping cranes have many different calls. They call out to one another when they are alarmed, to warn off intruders, and before takeoff and during flight. The most important call is the **unison call**. This is actually a combination of calls between a male and female crane. Whooping cranes use the unison call to claim territory and strengthen their pair-bond. Either the male or the female may start the call. The mate usually joins in right away. The male's call is lower-pitched, louder, and longer than the female's call. Biologists can tell male and female cranes apart by the pitches of their calls.

Crane Chicks

Although young cranes can swim soon after they are born, they do not learn to fly until they are about 80 days old.

Opposite: Tiny whooping crane chicks are completely dependent on their parents for food, warmth, and protection.

Captive whooping crane chicks are often fed with a hand puppet that looks like an adult whooping crane.

Whooping cranes are excellent parents. Cranes build their nest in an area that will be safe from predators. Once the female lays her eggs, both parents keep the eggs warm and safe from predators.

Both parents also care for the chicks. They feed them, keep them warm at night, and guard them from danger. The new whooper chicks are curious about their world. They wobble around on shaky legs and peck at everything. Although young cranes can swim soon after they are born, they do not learn to fly until they are about 80 days old.

WHOOPING CRANES

The Nest

Whoopers like to build their nests in the same area each spring. The nests are usually located in small lakes, ponds, or wet meadows. Whoopers use bulrushes and other plants to make their nests. The cranes build their nest in water that is 5.6 to 11.2 inches (14 to 28 cm) deep. A nest surrounded by water helps protect the eggs and chicks from predators. The nests are about 2.5 to 6 feet (.75 to 1.8 m) in diameter. They are raised up 2 to 14 inches (5 to 35 cm) above the water level.

Whooping crane nests are usually in very isolated areas that give the parents a good view of their surroundings.

Eggs

Whooping cranes usually lay two eggs, two days apart. The eggs are light brown with dark purplish-brown spots. They are about 4 inches (10.1 cm) long, 2.5 inches (6.3 cm) wide, and they each weigh about 6.2 ounces (176 g).

The whooper parents sit on the eggs to keep them warm. This is known as **incubating** the eggs. The parents also turn the eggs several times each day. This helps to prevent the growing chicks from sticking to the insides of their shells. While one parent sits on the nest, the other feeds or rests nearby and will chase or lure away any predators or intruders.

The eggs are incubated for 29 to 30 days. Since the eggs are not laid at the same time, they usually hatch a day apart.

24

Care

For the first three to four days, chicks do not move very far from their nest. During this time, both parents and young return to the nest at night. Although the crane family leaves the nest after about four days, they will stay within 1.1 miles (1.8 km) of the nest site for the next 16 days.

Parents feed their chicks constantly. If two chicks are hatched, only one chick usually survives. This may be due in part to a shortage of food in the whooping crane nesting area. All birds nest within a certain range that is best for their species. If they try to breed outside this range, there may not be enough appropriate food. Some biologists believe that Wood Buffalo National Park is at or near the northern edge of the whooping cranes' nesting range. If this is the case, the amount of food available in the park may be too low to allow for the survival of more than one chick per family. The birds are forced to nest in this area because other areas, which may have more food, also have more people.

The parents continue to feed the chicks even after the young cranes have learned how to fly. This care continues during the fall migration and throughout the winter. As the winter progresses, the young cranes become better at finding food for themselves. The following spring, many young whoopers migrate north with their parents. Once the family reaches the nesting grounds, the parents begin to nest again, and the young cranes fend for themselves.

Whooping crane chicks are fed and defended by both parents. The darker color of the chicks makes them difficult to see. This helps protect them from predators until they learn how to fly.

Imprinting

Like many other birds, newly-hatched whooping cranes form a strong bond to the first creature that cares for them. This process is called **imprinting**. In the wild, young chicks imprint on the sound and sight of their natural parents. Biologists think that imprinting may even begin before hatching. Chicks that are just about to hatch begin to make peeping sounds while they are still in the egg. The parents hear these sounds and answer them. Once the chick has hatched and can see its parents, the bond grows stronger.

Chicks recognize these older cranes as their own kind. This process is an important part of the crane's life. The new whoopers look to their parents for food and protection. They follow their parents around, and learn what to eat and how to respond to animals and to conditions in their environment. When a whooper is ready to mate, it will search for a partner that resembles its parents.

Imprinting helps a young whooper chick learn how to behave like a whooping crane.

Imprinting on Humans

The urge to imprint is very strong. If the parents are not present, a young chick will imprint on something else. This is a problem in cases where whooping cranes have been raised in captivity. In the 1970s, biologists discovered that captive-bred whoopers imprinted on humans. These birds were unfit to release in the wild. The captive birds did not know how to behave like wild whooping cranes.

The costume that biologists wear when they are with crane chicks does not really make humans look like whooping cranes, but it does disguise the human face and body.

Now biologists wear a costume whenever they are with captive whooper chicks. In this way, the chicks do not imprint on the human figure.

Chicks also imprint on sounds, so humans do not speak while around chicks. Instead, they play tapes of whooping cranes making mothering sounds. At the International Crane Foundation, stuffed adult cranes are placed with the young chicks. These adults have been stuffed in a crouching position with their wings open, so the chicks can huddle under them.

Development

Baby Chicks

Newly-hatched whooping crane chicks are covered in soft, fluffy, reddish feathers known as **down**. The chicks are quite small—barely the size of an adult robin. The eyes of adult whoopers are yellow, but whooper chicks have gray-blue eyes.

When a whooping crane first hatches, it has an **egg tooth** on the tip of its beak. The egg tooth is not really a tooth, but is a small, rough knob that helps the chick break through its hard eggshell. The egg tooth falls off within a few days of hatching.

Chicks are always hungry. They call often, begging their parents for food. Adult whoopers crush crabs, insects, or other foods with their beaks before offering the meal to their chick. Young whoopers develop their own hunting skills through practice. They peck at small bugs, grasses, and even their parents' legs. However, these young cranes rarely manage to catch anything.

Crane chicks grow very quickly. They can grow as much as one inch (2.5 cm) in a single day.

During the first few weeks after hatching, crane chicks and their parents usually stay within about a mile of their nesting area.

Juvenile Cranes

It can take about 100 days for whooping cranes to develop their juvenile plumage. Baby down is replaced by white feathers that are spotted with a cinnamon color. The heads of these young cranes are also covered in feathers. Cranes do not display their red patch until they get their adult plumage.

Until a juvenile crane, called a colt, learns how to fly, it is at danger from predators such as wolves. Flight is always a bird's best defense.

Learning to fly can be difficult. Even when the youngsters manage to get off the ground, they still have to land again. Young cranes have even been observed crash-landing into trees!

By their second autumn, whooping cranes **molt**, losing their juvenile plumage and getting their adult plumage. Their eyes lighten to yellow, and the birds show the distinctive black markings and red patch on their heads.

Although a whooper may pair off when it is two years old, it will not be ready to mate until it is three to five years old.

Habitat

Opposite: The whooping crane's summer nesting grounds are in Wood Buffalo National Park, in Canada.

Wetland habitat provides many food sources and nest sites. If you look closely, you can see a whooping crane nest in the center of this photograph.

Whooping cranes live in wetlands. Wetlands are habitats that have many marshes, streams, and ponds, as well as moisture in the soil.

The whooping crane's winter grounds in Texas have many ponds, rivers, and salt flats. A salt flat is a type of habitat that ranges from dry sandy areas to shallow pools of salty water.

The crane's summer nesting grounds are located in northern Canada. Whoopers spend about 4.5 months in their summer range. This region is also filled with shallow ponds and rivers. Cattails, bulrushes, and other plants grow along the edges of these ponds. The plants provide good protection for whooping crane nests.

Whooping Crane Territories

Winter

Whooping cranes establish their winter territories as soon as they reach the winter grounds. The size of a winter territory is about 0.7 square miles (1.7 sq km). The ideal territory includes ponds, bays, and salt flats. This variety allows cranes to feed on the many different animals that live in each habitat. A pair of cranes will defend their winter territory until spring migration.

Whooping cranes must migrate to a warm climate each winter. They cannot look for food on snow-covered ground and ice-covered ponds.

Summer

A whooper pair's summer territory is larger than their winter territory. The cranes need more room in the summer to find enough food to raise a chick successfully. In areas with lots of crane pairs, a summer territory can range from 1.3 to 1.7 square miles (3.2 to 4.2 sq km). Crane pairs that nest in isolated areas may have territories of 4.8 to 7.7 square miles (12 to 18.9 sq km).

Whooping cranes usually claim the same summer territory each year. During this time, the whooper population is spread out. Cranes will defend their territory if necessary, but even visual contact with other cranes is rare. Whoopers probably keep their distance from other pairs through vocal calls.

Wildlife Biologists Talk About Whooping Cranes

Robert P. Allen

"When you do spot a whooping crane, you wonder how you could mistake it for anything else.... It looks like a great, flightless, prehistoric bird, prancing about over the mud flats."

Robert P. Allen was a biologist who has worked with the National Audubon Society. Working in Aransas, Texas, he was the first person to study whooping cranes. He has written several important scientific books about whooping cranes.

Ernie Kuyt

"Many of the cooperators [of the whooping crane migration study] unfortunately could not witness the glorious spectacle of migrating whooping cranes, but their contributions were as important as those of the privileged crews who flew with the cranes."

Ernie Kuyt is a retired biologist who worked for the Canadian Wildlife Service. He has spent over 25 years studying wild whooping cranes and working for their survival. He has authored and edited many papers and books about the cranes.

Tom Stehn

"When I see a whooping crane in the marsh at Aransas, fully erect, glaring at an intruder and trumpeting an alarm call that can be heard up to 2 miles away, there is no doubt in my mind that the marsh belongs to the whoopers. It is our responsibility to keep that marsh unchanged so that the whoopers will continue to survive."

Tom Stehn works for the United States Fish and Wildlife Service in the Aransas area.

How to Spot a Whooping Crane

There are several North American birds that can be mistaken for whooping cranes. Examine the following key characteristics so that you can tell the difference.

Whooping Cranes

Whoopers are wading birds, with long legs and necks. When standing, they are over 5 feet (1.5 m) tall. When whooping cranes fly, their long legs trail, and their extended necks are easily visible.

American White Pelicans

American white pelicans are swimming birds. Their bill is long, large, and orange-yellow in color. They have a large throat pouch for catching fish. When a pelican flies, its neck is folded back on its shoulders. Like whooping cranes, pelicans use thermals to fly.

Snow Geese

Snow geese are waterfowl. They have short legs and webbed feet that allow them to swim easily through the water. In flight, their legs do not extend beyond their tails. Snow geese migrate in huge, noisy flocks.

Tundra Swans

Like cranes, tundra swans fly with their long necks extended. Their legs, however, do not extend beyond their tails in flight. In addition, their primaries are white rather than black, like the whooping crane. The birds tend to fly in flocks of 45 to 60 birds.

Wood Storks

Wood storks are found in wetlands, and they are similar in shape to whooping cranes. The trick to telling the two birds apart is in their markings. Wood storks are white, but their heads are black, and their beaks are curved downward. Both their primary and secondary wing feathers are black.

Sandhill Cranes

Sandhill cranes have the same body shape as whooping cranes. They also fly in the same way, with their legs trailing behind and their necks extended. However, sandhill cranes are not pure white, and they lack the black head markings of a whooper. In addition, sandhill cranes usually fly in much larger flocks than whooping cranes.

Food

Opposite: Crabs are an important food source for whooping cranes on their winter grounds.

While whooping cranes eat some plant foods, shellfish and insects make up the largest part of their diet. Whoopers hunt crabs and other water animals by wading after them until they can catch them with their beaks.

Whoopers are **omnivores**, which means they eat both animal and plant foods. On their winter grounds, a whooping crane's favorite foods include the numerous blue crabs, clams, and mud shrimp that live in the salt flats. Crayfish, marine worms, snails, berries, acorns, insects, and shellfish are all part of the whooper's winter diet. During the winter, whooping cranes feed on at least 28 different kinds of animal foods, and 17 kinds of plant foods.

On their summer grounds, whooping cranes may feed on water snails, clams, leeches, frogs, garter snakes, small fish, mice, and the larvae of dragonflies, damselflies, and other insects.

Finding Food

Many of the whooping crane's favorite foods, such as crabs, shrimp, and clams, live in shallow ponds in the soft mud. The whooper wades slowly into the pond, lowering its head to look for signs of burrows or tracks. The cranes use their long, strong beaks to stab at their prey. If the clams are deep in the mud, a whooper may also use its beak to dig them out. Whoopers are very good at catching crabs and clams. A biologist once saw a female catch 32 clams in just 30 minutes!

Like other birds, whoopers do not have teeth. This means that they cannot chew their food. Most prey is swallowed whole. In one gulp, a whooper can swallow a clam that is 4 inches (10 cm) long and 1.5 inches (4 cm) in diameter. If a creature is too large to gulp down at once, the whooper will bring it to the shore and peck it into bite-sized pieces.

When whooping cranes stop at their staging area during fall migration, they feed on grains left over from the harvest. Barley, wheat, and corn are important foods for the cranes during their staging period. It is on the staging grounds that young whoopers really begin to learn how to find food for themselves.

The whooping crane's long, powerful beak is used to catch and dig up food. The crane's beak is also useful for poking through mud or even cow dung to find insects.

The Food Web

A food web shows how energy, or food, is passed from one living thing to another. Many of the whooping crane's foods, such as insects and frogs, are especially vulnerable to changes in their environment. Insects are sensitive to temperature changes. Frogs will not survive in polluted waters. All animals in a web are affected by the health of the other animals. How would the whooping crane's food web be affected if one link, such as insects, suddenly disappeared?

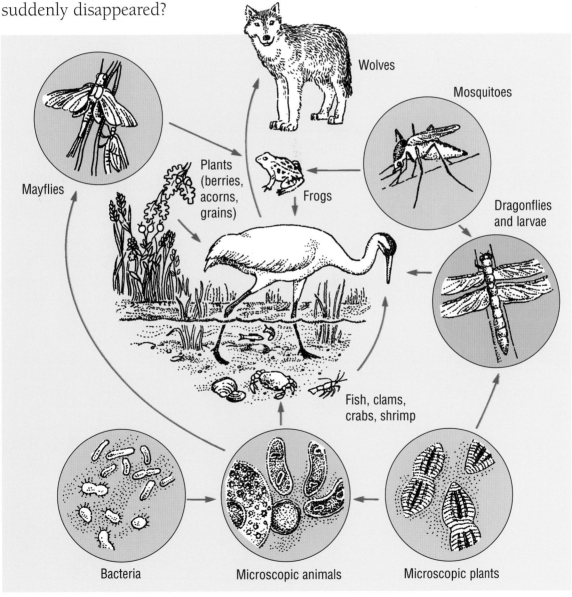

Competition

Whoopers have lost most of their traditional nesting grounds, as well as some of their staging grounds due to human activities.

Opposite: Much of the whooping crane's traditional territory has been turned into farmland.

The migration route between the southern wintering grounds and northern nesting grounds can be dangerous for whoopers because they come into contact with human settlements.

Competition between whooping cranes is not a serious problem. Although cranes can be aggressive toward their whooper neighbors, direct competition is rarely necessary because there are so few birds.

Adult cranes are often tolerant of subadults in their territory. Whooping cranes are also tolerant of most other bird species. However, there may be some competition between the whoopers and sandhill cranes over nest sites.

The whooping crane's most serious competitors are human beings. As human development has expanded, whooper habitat has shrunk. Whoopers will not live close to human settlements. Whoopers have lost most of their traditional nesting grounds, as well as some of their staging grounds due to human activities.

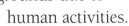

Competing with Other Whoopers

On both their summer and winter grounds, an adult whooping crane pair establishes its territory in the same marsh as the previous year. Although whoopers will defend their territory against intruders, competition between well-established pairs of cranes is rare. The male crane is usually responsible for chasing off any trespassers. He flies toward the strange crane, calling loudly. The intruder is most often a subadult. Before the territorial crane gets close enough to attack, the younger crane usually backs off and leaves the area.

On the winter grounds, the amount of competition between adult and subadult whoopers may depend on the individual cranes. Some pairs are quick to defend their territory and chase away young intruders. Other whoopers do not mind their subadult neighbors as much. In many cases, these neighbors are also relatives. Young adult whoopers often establish their own winter territories beside their parents' territory. In rare cases, a whooper pair will allow small flocks of subadults on their winter range. On the nesting grounds, however, a crane pair will chase off all intruding whoopers.

While one crane keeps the eggs warm, the other stays close by, ready to warn away intruders.

Relationships with Other Animals

Whooping cranes and sandhill cranes occupy many of the same areas. Although there is some competition between the two species for nest sites, they do not normally compete for food. Sandhill cranes prefer eating plants, so they usually look for food on land. Whooping cranes prefer eating aquatic animals, so they usually look for food in ponds and marshes. Here, a whooper may compete with an American bittern, another wading bird that also eats aquatic animals.

Whooping cranes also share their habitat with a number of predators. These predators rarely catch a whooping crane. Whooper parents are on guard against predators at all times, so their chicks are usually safe. While a predator may succeed in killing a sick or injured adult crane, biologists have never seen a predator take a healthy adult whooper.

Whooping cranes and sandhill cranes usually live together peacefully. Biologists have even used sandhill cranes as foster parents for young whooping cranes.

Lynx, black bears, wolves, and golden eagles may make a meal of a whooping crane chick if they get a chance.

Competing with Humans

Competition between whooping cranes and humans began in the early 1900s. As human populations grew, whooper populations were squeezed into smaller areas. In the northern United States and southern Canada, which were once common staging areas for whoopers, many prairie fields and meadows were drained and plowed to build farms. Most of the whooping crane's traditional nesting grounds have now disappeared.

Wetlands have also been affected by human development. Wetlands are essential for whooping crane migration. These marshes and wet meadows provide a place for whooping cranes to feed and rest during their long journey south. Dams and other irrigation projects have drained many of these important wetlands.

Irrigation projects are partly responsible for the loss of whooping crane habitat. They divert water from some of the important wetland areas that provide the cranes with resting grounds and food.

Decline in Population

Whooping crane populations have never been large. When European settlers came to North America, whooper populations probably numbered about 1,300 to 1,400 birds. At this time, whooping cranes ranged across the continent. When humans began settling the prairies, however, whooping cranes retreated to more remote areas.

At the same time, hunters began to kill the birds. Whooping cranes are large and impressive-looking. Hunters prized the cranes as trophies and as food. In addition, many museums and collectors paid to get whooping crane skins and eggs for their exhibits. In the late 1800s and early 1900s, 90 percent of the whooping crane population either died from hunting or failed to breed successfully due to habitat loss. Today, whooping cranes are a protected species. It is against the law to harass or kill a whooper, although hunters sometimes shoot the cranes by accident.

Hunters are just one of the hazards that whoopers face. During migration, the cranes sometimes collide with power lines, or get trapped in barbed-wire fences. In addition, a drought in the summer grounds can reduce the number of good nest sites and affect feeding areas. When this happens, crane chicks may not survive to maturity.

This photo of a dead sandhill crane shows the danger that power lines pose to crane populations during migration.

Folklore

Biologist Paul Johnsgard once wrote that "cranes are the stuff of magic." Cranes have captured people's imaginations around the world. Wherever they live in the wild, cranes appear in local folktales and legends. Their dances have inspired human dancers from cultures in Australia, Siberia, and the Mediterranean. Their wing bones have been made into whistles to encourage bravery in Crow and Cheyenne cultures. The crane's ability to fly over long distances has also been greatly admired. In Greece, a crane's wing was used as a charm to fight exhaustion.

In Oriental myth and art, cranes have long been symbols of long life, faithfulness, and happiness. Many legends were told in which cranes helped or rewarded worthy humans. When people died, their souls were said to ride up to heaven on the back of a crane.

Opposite: The Shotokan school of karate has several positions known as "crane on a rock."

The image of the dancing or bowing crane is common in Japanese culture.

Folklore History

There have been stories told about whooping cranes throughout history. Some stories told of cranes swallowing heavy stones before their flight, to keep the birds from being tossed around by strong winds. Other tales suggested that a crane's feathers, like human hair, grew white with age. In the southern United States, people believed that a crane circling three times over a house meant that someone in the house would die. The Inuit of the Bering Sea believed that circling cranes were looking for humans to steal. Although science has since disproved these stories, cranes still have the power to fire the human imagination.

Cranes appear in many ancient Greek and Roman stories. In one myth, the god Mercury invents the letters of the Greek alphabet by watching the changing patterns of a flight of cranes. The letter lambda, *as shown, is thought to be one of the letters invented by Mercury.*

Folktales

Many folktales and stories tell why the crane looks the way it does. Others are tales of clever cranes or cranes that reward people for their kindness. Here are a few crane tales you might enjoy:

People Helping Cranes

A boy and his grandfather save the life of a wounded crane.

Byars, Betsy. *The House of Wings*. New York: The Viking Press, 1972.

How and Why Stories

Find out why the crane has such a long beak in an Australian story about a crane and an emu.

Leach, Maria. *How the People Sang the Mountains Up*. New York: Viking, 1967.

Cranes Helping People

A crane rewards a poor woodcutter after the man frees him from a trap.

Matsutani Miyoko. *The Crane's Reward*. London: Adam & Charles Black, 1966.

A crane helps fugitives across a stream by letting them cross on his leg. The clever crane then drops the pursuers into the river.

Heady, Eleanor. *Sage Smoke: Tales of the Shoshoni-Bannock Indians*. Chicago: Follett, 1973.

Clever Cranes

Two stories in this collection tell of clever cranes. In the first story, a crane tricks some fish into being carried from one pond to another. The second story tells of a crane that removes a bone from a lion's throat.

Jacobs, Joseph. *Indian Folk and Fairy Tales*. New York: Putnam, 1968.

A Cree story tells how Crane was rewarded with a red head after carrying Rabbit to the moon.

Belting, Natalia. *The Long-Tailed Bear and Other Indian Legends*. Indianapolis: Bobbs-Merrill, 1961.

Sadako and the Paper Cranes

Sadako Sasaki was a girl who lived in Japan. She was only two years old when the atomic bomb was dropped on Hiroshima on August 6, 1945. Years later, she developed a type of cancer called leukemia as a result of radiation from the bomb. As she lay sick in the hospital, a friend told her the story of the crane. In Japanese folklore, the crane is supposed to live for 1,000 years. The legends say that a sick person who folds 1,000 paper cranes will become healthy again.
After hearing the story, Sadako began to fold cranes.

Unfortunately, Sadako's leukemia was very severe. She managed to fold only 644 paper cranes before she died. She was just 12 years old.

Her classmates folded the remaining 356 cranes. When Sadako was buried, the 1,000 cranes were buried with her. A statue of Sadako was placed in Hiroshima Peace Park. Each year on Peace Day, August 6th, Japanese schoolchildren place paper cranes beneath Sadako's statue.

Visitors to the statue of Sadako in the Hiroshima Peace Park often leave behind colorful origami cranes.

HOW TO FOLD A PAPER CRANE

1. Crease a square piece of paper diagonally from the left and right corners, then turn the paper over, and crease it in half both ways.

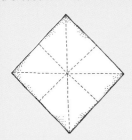

2. Bring the four corners together, and press the flaps down to form a square.

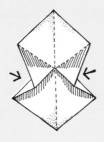

3. Make three creases along dotted lines ABC by first aligning CX and CY with the central crease.

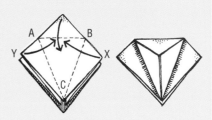

4. Lift up and fully extend point C, using the top sheet only. Hold the lower sheets down with your finger. Pull point C back all the way, using the AB crease. Press flat. Turn over, repeating step 3.

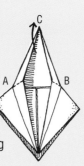

5. Fold the sides inward, back and front.

6. Bring points D and E together in front and F and G together behind.

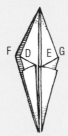

7. Fold up along the crease at the dotted line, back and front.

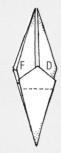

8. Bring points F and D together in front and G and E together behind. Press flat.

9. Pinch the base with one hand, while pulling the neck out slightly. Pinch the base with your left hand while pulling out the tail with your right hand.

10. Fold down and pull out the beak, pinching the head. Pull the wings out and down.

To inflate the body of the crane, blow into the hole at the bottom.

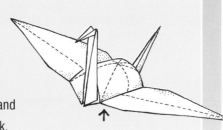

Whooping Crane Distribution

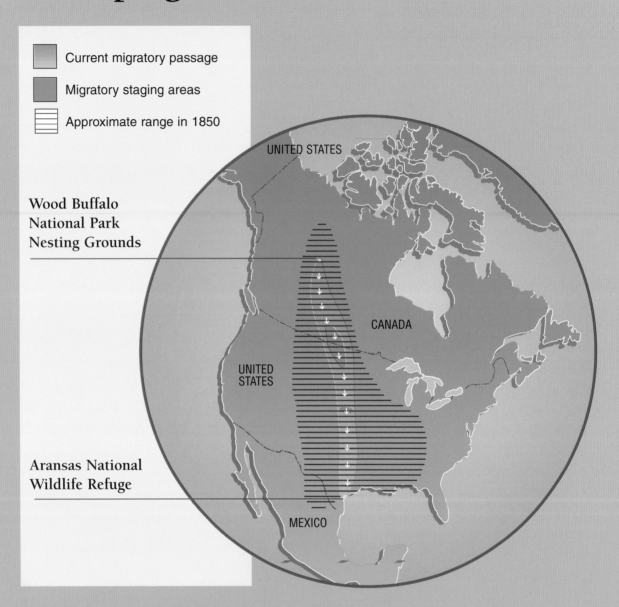

- Current migratory passage
- Migratory staging areas
- Approximate range in 1850

Wood Buffalo
National Park
Nesting Grounds

Aransas National
Wildlife Refuge

UNITED STATES

CANADA

UNITED
STATES

MEXICO

Status

While hunting and illegal egg collecting have reduced the number of whooping cranes, the worst problems are caused by habitat destruction.

W hile hunting and illegal egg collecting have reduced the number of whooping cranes, the worst problems for cranes are caused by habitat destruction. In 1937 the United States Fish and Wildlife Service took action to help the cranes. They created the Aransas National Wildlife Refuge in Texas. The refuge protects the whooping cranes' winter grounds. This protection was an important step, but it did not protect the birds in the summer. At that time, nobody even knew where the cranes spent the summer.

Biologists discovered the whoopers' summer nesting grounds in 1954. Fortunately, the cranes were found to be nesting in Wood Buffalo National Park—an area that was already protected.

Due to successful conservation efforts by biologists in the United States and Canada, the whooping crane's population has shown a steady increase since 1940.

THE WHOOPING CRANE'S COMEBACK	
Year	Population Size
1940	22
1950	34
1960	33
1970	56
1980	76
1990	146
1991	132
1992	136
1993	143
1994	133
1995	156

The Whooping Crane Recovery Program

The survival of the migratory whooping crane population is partially due to a joint program between Canada and the United States. The Whooping Crane Recovery Program works to save fertile whooping crane eggs.

The program involves locating whooping crane nests and examining the eggs. Birds sometimes lay eggs that are infertile. This means that the chicks inside have not formed properly and will not hatch. As part of the recovery program, biologists decided to make sure that each breeding pair of cranes had one fertile egg in their nest.

Whooping cranes usually lay two eggs, but even if both hatch successfully, it is rare for both chicks to survive to adulthood. Biologists decided to remove the second eggs from the nests. They then tested the eggs to see if they were fertile. If a whooper pair produced an infertile egg, it was replaced with a healthy one from another pair. In this way, each set of whooper parents would have a healthy egg, and each chick that hatched would have a better chance of survival.

A whooping crane chick begins to break out of its shell. Under the recovery program, whooper chicks are more likely to grow up to be healthy adult cranes.

For the recovery program, whooping crane nests were located by plane and noted on a map during April and May. At the end of May, teams of biologists flew to the nesting grounds by helicopter to test and collect whooping crane eggs. Taking an egg from a whooping crane's nest can be risky. The parent cranes usually become upset at the human interference. Some people worried that the cranes might even abandon the remaining egg. Biologists are very careful about taking eggs from the birds' nests. To date, not a single whooping crane pair has abandoned its nest as a result of the biologists' work.

Crane biologist Ernie Kuyt found that a wool sock was a perfect way to move whooping crane eggs.

When biologists take an egg from a nest, they put it in a wool sock to protect it and keep it warm. In the helicopter, the egg is placed in an incubator. Some eggs are immediately placed in whooper nests, while others are flown to captive rearing facilities the following day. These chicks are raised in captivity. Eventually biologists hope to release these captive-bred birds into the wild.

Problems with Captive-bred Cranes

Using eggs collected by whooping crane biologists, three captive flocks of whoopers have now been established. They are located at the Patuxent Wildlife Research Center in Maryland, the International Crane Foundation in Wisconsin, and the Calgary Zoo in Calgary, Canada.

One of the original goals of the whooping crane recovery program was to establish a second migratory group of whooping cranes. Biologists wanted this second group to be separate from the existing flock that lives in Wood Buffalo Park and the Aransas National Wildlife Refuge. If a natural disaster wiped out one group of cranes, the other would still survive.

Many cranes have been raised in captive facilities by humans. Some whoopers have even been raised by sandhill crane foster parents. However, even after 30 years, not one of these birds has been added to the wild. There are many reasons for this. Captive breeding is really a last attempt to save a species. In the case of whooping cranes, it often results in birds that do not know how to behave like whooping cranes. Some do not breed because they fail to recognize other whoopers as potential mates. Others never learn to recognize predators as a danger. These captive-bred birds cannot be released because they do not know how to lead a normal life in the wild.

Biologists make sure that crane chicks do not imprint on humans by wearing costumes. However, cranes raised in captivity may never learn to find food or to mate.

Viewpoints

Should more money be spent on whooping crane recovery programs?

For more than 30 years, the American and Canadian governments have spent a large amount of money on conservation efforts for the whooping crane. At the same time, other species have become endangered, and money is needed to save them. There is seldom enough money for all of the animals. Should more money be spent on whooping crane recovery programs, or should the money now go toward saving other species?

PRO

1 Humans have destroyed whooping crane habitat to create farms and towns. Power lines and barbed-wire fences have killed migrating cranes. Humans have a responsibility to save the crane, because human actions have caused their population to decline.

2 Whooping cranes are one of the rarest and most magnificent birds in North America. If we do not try to save them, they will become extinct, and we will never be able to get them back.

CON

1 Some animals become extinct naturally. Whooping cranes were never very numerous. It is possible that the cranes were on the brink of extinction before humans moved into their habitat. We should not spend money trying to save a species that was already going to become extinct.

2 The whooping crane is not the only endangered species worthy of conservation efforts. We have spent significant amounts of money on the cranes, and these efforts have shown some success. It is time to spend conservation money on other animals in danger of extinction.

What You Can Do

By learning more about whooping cranes, you can make better decisions about how to help them. Write to a government organization or a conservation group. You can also follow the whoopers' amazing migration route on the Internet.

Conservation Groups

UNITED STATES

International Crane Foundation
E-11376 Shady Lane Road
Baraboo, WI
53913-9778

Whooping Crane Conservation Association
1007 Carmel Avenue
Lafayette, LA
70501

CANADA

Nature Conservancy Canada
4th floor, 110 Eglington Avenue, W.
Toronto, Ontario
M4R 2G5

Canadian Nature Federation
1 Nicholas Street
Suite 520
Ottawa, Ontario
K1N 7B7

Government

UNITED STATES

United States Fish and Wildlife Service
1849 C Street NW
Washington, D.C.
20240

Aransas National Wildlife Refuge
P.O. Box 100
Austwell, TX
77950

Whoopers on the Internet

You can learn more about whooping cranes on the Internet. The *Journey North* site allows you to follow the whooping cranes as they make their annual spring migration to Wood Buffalo National Park. For more information on *Journey North*, visit their home page at:
http://www.learner.org/k12

You can also contact *Journey North* by e-mail at: **jn-register-info@learner.org**

Twenty Fascinating Facts

1 Whooping cranes are the tallest and one of the rarest birds in North America.

2 A whooping crane's loud, trumpeting call can be heard from over 2 miles (3.2 km) away.

3 Whooping cranes have flexible necks that help them find food easily. They have up to 20 separate neck bones. Humans only have 7 neck bones.

4 Birds that make the loudest sounds have long, coiled windpipes. Stretched out, the whooping crane's windpipe is 58 inches (147 cm) long. This is the same length as the entire bird!

5 Whooping cranes have thin, hollow bones. These light bones make it possible for them to fly.

6 Adult whoopers and older chicks usually sleep standing up, with one leg raised and held close to their bodies.

7 Whooping cranes mate for life. If a crane's mate dies, the remaining crane will usually choose a new partner.

8 Subadult cranes usually live and migrate in small flocks of other subadults.

13 In a process known as imprinting, newly hatched whooping cranes form a strong bond to the creature that cares for them. Young chicks in the wild always imprint on their natural parents, but captive chicks can also imprint on other birds or humans.

9 Biologists can tell if a whooper is male or female by the pitch of its call. In addition, when calling in unison, the male crane often holds its wings so the black tips are visible. The female usually does not.

11 Migrating whoopers usually fly at about 1,950 feet (600 m) above the ground, although they may fly even higher. One crane family was observed flying at 6,338 feet (1,950 m).

14 The whooping crane's favorite foods are crabs, shrimp, clams, grains, and frogs. Whoopers also eat snakes, berries, acorns, and insects. They have even been known to stalk ducklings. Biologists reported that one whooping crane killed and ate a red-winged blackbird, while another ate an American bittern.

10 The whoopers' migration route is over 2,485 miles (4,000 km) long. The migration can take anywhere from 10 to 40 days in the spring, and about 50 days in the fall.

12 Whooping cranes do not learn to fly until they are about 80 days old. This gives them about a month to practice flying before they have to make the long journey to the winter grounds.

15 Both whooping crane parents take turns incubating the eggs. While one crane sits on the nest, the other watches for predators, rests, or feeds nearby.

16 In Oriental art, cranes and pine trees are often pictured together. Both pine trees and cranes symbolize happiness, long life, faithfulness, and love. It was said that old pine trees sometimes became cranes.

17 A nest of eggs is called a clutch. Whooping cranes usually lay clutches of two eggs.

18 Whooper chicks break out of their shell by using their egg tooth. Other than birds, only snakes and lizards have this kind of tooth.

19 In Japanese folklore, the crane is supposed to live for 1,000 years. Legends say that a sick person who folds 1,000 paper cranes will become healthy again.

20 By 1940 there were only 16 whooping cranes left in the wild. Now the wild whooping crane population has grown to over 150 cranes. The most serious threat to whooping crane survival is habitat destruction. Although the cranes' summer and winter grounds are protected, much of their migration habitat, including the fall staging area, is not. The best way to help the whooping cranes is to preserve their habitat.

Glossary

down: A covering of soft, fluffy feathers

egg tooth: A small, rough knob on a chick's beak that helps it break out of its shell. The egg tooth falls off after a few days.

imprint: A process in which newly-hatched birds form a strong bond to their parents

incubate: To sit on eggs in order to hatch them by the warmth of the body

migrate: A regular, seasonal movement from a winter range to a summer range, and back again

molt: When a bird loses its feathers and replaces them with new ones

omnivore: An animal that eats both plants and animals

pair-bonding: The process in which whooping cranes choose their mates

plumage: A bird's feathers

preen: When a bird grooms itself by smoothing and straightening its feathers

primaries: A bird's long, main wing feathers

staging area: An area where whooping cranes traditionally stop to rest and eat during their migration

subadult: Cranes that are at least a year old, but are not yet old enough to mate

territorial: Being protective of one's home range

thermals: Columns, or bubbles, of warm air that rise up in the sky

unison call: A combination of calls between the male and female of a mated pair of cranes

wetlands: A habitat with many marshes, streams, and ponds, as well as moisture in the soil

Suggested Reading

Allen, R.P. *The Whooping Crane*. National Audubon Society. New York: Roy Press, 1952.

Coerr, Eleanor. *Sadako and the Thousand Paper Cranes*. New York: G.P. Putnam's Sons, 1977.

Johnsgard, Paul. *Crane Music: A Natural History of American Cranes*. Washington: Smithsonian Institution Press, 1991.

McNulty, Faith. *The Whooping Crane: The Bird That Defied Extinction*. New York: Dutton, 1966.

Patent, Dorothy Hinshaw. *The Whooping Crane: A Comeback Story*. New York: Houghton Mifflin Company, 1988.

Roop, Peter and Connie. *Seasons of the Cranes*. New York: Walker and Company, 1989.

Index